MW00883140

Today is Amealia's first day going to her new school. She is very scared. Amelia's mama tries to cheer her up, by listening to her favorite music, but it did not work.

Finally, they pulled up to the school. Amealia and her mama got out the car. They walked to the front door and the principal was waiting for her.

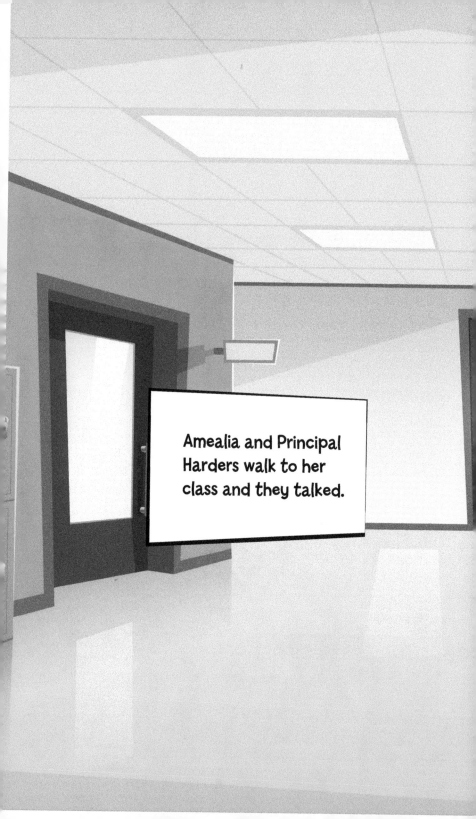

Amealia and Principal Harders walk to her class and they talked.

The school was bigger than her last school. It was a lot of kids. As, they got closer to her class she heard voices of students.

The door was wide open waiting for her.
As she walked in the students were playing
and the teacher was walking towards the door.

All the students gather on the carpet. Everyone looked at Amelia.

The students started finding their partners as Amealia stood aside. One of the students started walking toward her. The little girl started talking to Amealia.

Rosie and Amealia went to sit down. Amelia started talking a little more.

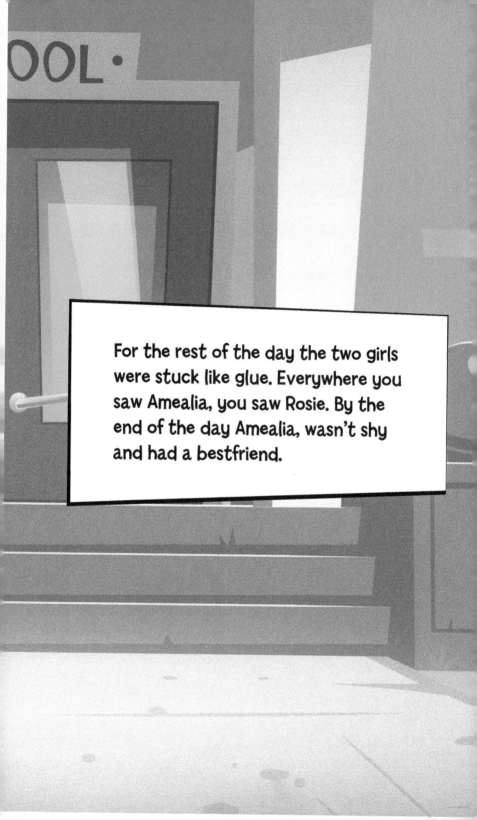

For the rest of the day the two girls were stuck like glue. Everywhere you saw Amealia, you saw Rosie. By the end of the day Amealia, wasn't shy and had a bestfriend.

CPSIA information can be obtained
at www.ICGtesting.com
Printed in the USA
BVHW061525020721
611064BV00024B/1656